We've Got a Mission!

Designed by Carol Leslie & Nadeem Zaidi

Photo credits: Fluffy clouds © Craig Aurness/Corbis; Grassy hill and fields © W. Cody/Corbis; Rustic stairwell © Melanie Acevedo/Botanica; Scenic view of a waterfall on Havasu Creek © Wilbur E. Garrett/National Geographi Farm, Peacham, Vermont, USA © Panoramic Images; Meadow of wildflowers © William A. Bake/Corbis; Fireweed Mendenhall Glacier, Juneau, Alaska, USA © Panoramic Images; Alpine landscape of lupine-covered meadow, Olympic Nationa Park, Washington © Darrell Gulin/Botanica; Fountain of Four Evangelists in central courtyard of San Juan Capistrano © Stephen Saks/Lonely Planet Images; Golf course, Manalee Bay, Lanai, Hawaii, USA © Panoramic Images; Landscap reflecting in lake, Norway © Howard Kingsnorth/zefa/Corbis; Regal lilies in garden © Mark Bolton/Corbis; Man standing at waterfall, Bavaria, Germany © Uli Wiesmeier/zefa/Corbis; Moeraki Boulders, stones on beach near Oamaru, Nev Zealand © Wilfried Krecichwost/zefa/Corbis; Tree frog sitting on a branch © Theo Allofs/zefa/Corbis; Vintgar Gorge, Slovenia © Roland Gerth/zefa/Corbis; Cascading by the wildflowers © Craig Tuttle/Corbis; Glacial erratics on prairi © Tom Bean/Corbis; Doorway of patriotic home © Strauss/Curtis/Corbis; Young man jumping out of water © Parque/zefa/Corbis; Shallow water at shore of lake © Ron Watts/Corbis; Upper Multnomah Falls © Craig Tuttle/Corbi Tree-frog tadpole © Michael & Patricia Fogden/Corbis; Red-eyed leaf-frog tadpoles © Michael & Patricia Fogden/Corbis; Western green tree frog leaping from tree trunk © David A. Northcott/Corbis; Serious bullfrog © Randy N Ury/Corbis; Snorkeling off Bora-Bora © Patrick Ward/Corbis; A chipmunk eats a nut © Taylor S. Kennedy/National Geographic; Black panther on a tree branch © John Conrad/Corbis; Eastern American chipmunk © Gary W. Carter/Corbi Brugmansia hangs over mixed floral bed © Marion Brenner/Botanica; A captive birdwing butterfly lands on a pink flower © Roy Toft/National Geographic; Close view of a blue and yellow glassy tiger butterfly on a pink flower © Timothy Laman/National Geographic; Panoramic view of field of poppies and wild flowers near Montchiello, Tuscany, Italy, Europe © Lee Frost/Robert Harding World Imagery; Chestnut trees in the autumn © Herbert Kehrer/zefa/Corbis; Butterflie flying © Thom Lang/Corbis; Three baby robins in a nest Wilmington, Delaware © Lisa J. Goodman/The Image Bank; Robin (Erithacus rubecula) © Pal Hermansen/The Image Bank; Close-up of the feather-shaped leaves of many gloss leaflets of the evergreen, slender palm Chamaedorea elegans, Neanthe Bella Dwarf mountain palm, Parlour palm © Dorling Kindersley/Dorling Kindersley; A chipmunk eats a nut © Taylor S. Kennedy/National Geographic; Man standing a waterfall, Bavaria, Germany © Uli Wiesmeier/zefa/Corbis; Red-bellied woodpecker sitting at a hole on the tree trunk © Markus Botzek/zefa/Corbis; Coral Pink Sand Dunes State Park, Utah © Massimo Mastrorillo/Corbis; Grasshopper © H. Zettl/zefa/Corbis; Eggs in bird's nest © Burke/Triolo Productions/Brand X Pictures; Bee zooming to Iceland poppy © Taesam Do/Botanica; Buffy fish-owl, Ketupa-ketupa, perched on a branch facing the viewer © Cyril Laubscher/Dorlir Kindersley; Wildflowers © Annie Griffiths Belt/National Geographic; Close view of a blue and yellow glassy tiger butterfly on a pink flower © Timothy Laman/National Geographic; Grand Teton Park, Wyoming, USA © Panoramic Image Teenage boy fishing at lake © Caterina Bernardi/zefa/Corbis; Butterfly Collection © G. Schuster/zefa/Corbis; Robin on branch © Christof Wermter/zefa/Corbis; Bat flying at night © F. Rauschenbach/zefa/Corbis; Owl © H Spichtinger/zefa/Corbis; Eastern American chipmunk examining a wild mushroom © Orion Press/Corbis; Little brown bat in flight © Joe McDonald/Corbis; Leaf-nosed bat flying in night © Joe McDonald/Corbis; Atlas moth above othe moths and butterflies © Darrell Gulin/Corbis; Meadow of wildflowers © William A. Bake/Corbis; Rolling green hills against sky © Terry W. Eggers/Corbis; Maize field and flowers © Gallo Images; Orange poppy sways © Botanica; Meadow of spring wildflowers, including California poppies (Eschscholzia californica) and owl's clover (Orthocarpus), Antelope Valley, California, USA © Visuals Unlimited; Baby bird in nest © The Image Bank; Fern Leaves © Iconica; Broken robin egg in empty bird's nest © Taxi; Leaves on branch © Photonica

Printed in Malaysia

ISBN 0-7868-5537-1

For more Disney Press fun, visit www.disneybooks.com

Music of the
Meadow

by Susan Ring
Illustrated by Katie Nix & Kelly Peterson

This is Rocket. He takes us anywhere we want to go. And you never know what special tool he'll use next to help us with our missions!

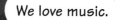

The meadow seems like a very quiet and calm place. But did you know that the meadow is filled with music?
And you can help us find it.
So come with us!
Let's go on an adventure. Let's explore the meadow together.

Welcome to the meadow. **Look! It's a bee!** It has come to visit. Listen…do you hear something? The bee is making a buzzing sound. Can you buzz like the bee?

Buzz

Buzz

Buzz!

Honeybees do a special *dance*.
That is how they tell the other bees
where the yummy nectar is.
What is your honeybee dance?

Look! It's a flower! It is very pretty. Listen…do you hear something? The flower sways and rustles softly in the wind. Can you sway like the flower?

Swaaayyy

Look! It's a stream! It is cool and clear. Listen…do you hear something? The water is swishing and splashing over the rocks. Can you swish and splash like the stream?

Rub your hands together.

Swish Swish Swish

Look! It's a frog! It is sitting near the water. Listen…do you hear something? The frog croaks to say hello. Can you croak like the frog?

Frogs start out as tiny tadpoles swimming in the water. Even when they are all grown up, they still like to swim.

Splash

Look! It's a chipmunk! It is eating a nut. Listen...do you hear something? The chipmunk is chewing. Can you chew and chomp like the chipmunk?

I like to eat nuts, too. Crunch, crunch, crunch.

Chipmunks got their name because they make a loud "chipping" sound. Can you "chip" like a chipmunk?

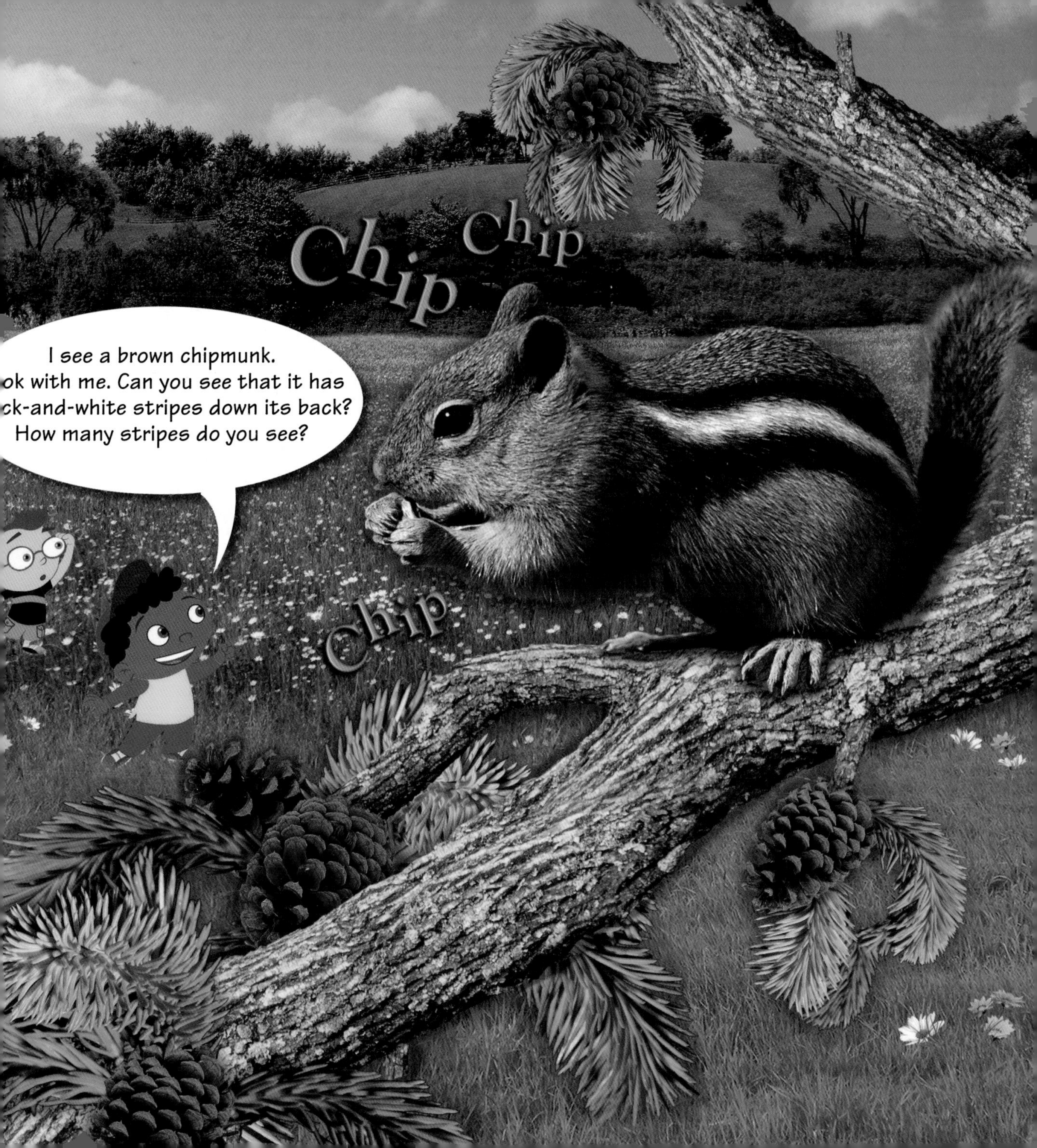

Look! It's a butterfly! It has landed on a bush. Listen…do you hear something? The butterfly is drinking. It sips sweet nectar from the flowers. *Slurp, slurp, slurp.* Can you slurp like the butterfly?

The butterfly has its own little built-in straw.

Slurp slurp Slurp

Someday this caterpillar will change into a beautiful butterfly.

Look! It's a bird and its babies! They are up in a tree. Listen…do you hear something? The bird is singing a sweet song. Can you sing like the bird?

Tap
Tap
Tap

I hear a *tap, tap, tap.* That's a woodpecker tapping at a tree. It is looking for bugs to eat. Can you tap, tap, tap along with it?

Oh, no! A baby bird has fallen out of the tree.

Don't worry! Rocket is putting the b bird back in the tree.

Look! It's a grasshopper! It is jumping in the grass. Listen…do you hear something? The grasshopper is chirping. *Chirp, chirp, chirp.* Can you chirp like the grasshopper?

Grasshoppers make their chirping sound by rubbing a leg over one of their wings.

chirp chirp chirp

Like many insects,
grasshoppers have six legs.
Their short front legs help them walk.
Their long back legs help them jump!
Ooops! There it goes!
Chirp
Chirp
Chirp

Look! It's sunset! Our day is ending. Listen…do you hear something? *Shhhhh.* Many parts of the meadow are sleeping. But others are just waking up! There are crickets chirping. Moths fluttering. Bats flapping. And owls saying *who, who, who.*

There's always a symphony here in the meadow!